AN EAGLE'S EYE

DEATH SCENE FROM ABOVE

SANDI HOOVER

Contents

Chapter 1
SUNDAY

Lanny ran three steps and leapt off the cliff atop the nearly eleven-thousand-foot peak of the Sandia Mountains sheltering the eastern side of Albuquerque.

"Oof!" Once again the sudden forty-foot drop made her gasp, but the hang glider's wing stabilized, and she grinned as she leveled out and got her feet into the harness behind her.

She spoke quietly into the phone mic clipped at chin level. "Gary, I figure you're already down from the crest, and I'll see you at the soccer field."

Soaring was Lanny's escape from the rigors of the day or the week. She thrilled to that quiet realm, the barest swish of air over the wing, like a warm benediction, heightening the sense of motion. Silently she sped at altitude, paralleling the rough-edged face of the mountains, hunting for ridge lift, concentrating on her breath, relaxing into the harness, settling her mind and body for the morning's flight. The sharp aroma of pines clinging to those jagged slopes teased her nose as a whiff of air brushed her face. *Pffst,* blowing a strand of hair out of her mouth, *dratted hair, gonna get it cut short,* she vowed again to change its length.

Gary broke into her musing. "Gotcha, Lanny. I was headed down the road before you even got off. Your signal's good and clear. I'm already hustling south on Highway 14. Keep in touch so I know where to meet you in case the spot changes."

"Roger that. Now just playing with the wind, and heading south toward Albuquerque, so the soccer field off Tramway should still be best."

Remaining highly focused, since soaring demanded precision, she glanced down to watch for emergency landing opportunities should she need one and scanned the ground for movement simply because she was interested in what happened there. Having been the object of a Cooper's Hawk's ire, she was alert to motion close at hand, moving her head slowly so the *Go Pro* camera attached to her helmet would capture a good video picture. She learned this technique through hard experience when looking at the video after an earlier flight made her nauseous.

"Gary, can you still hear me? Are you enjoying this beautiful Sunday morning? I can hear church bells while I'm watching the sun peeping over the crest—lighting the west side of the valley, but the rest, including me, is still in shadow. As we anticipated, the west breeze is creating lift here, so I'm sure to make the rendezvous."

Her blue and gray hang glider followed the mountain face. She leaned, tilting the wing to more closely approach the foothills in front of the range. Looking at the instrument on her wrist, *1000 feet AGL, good,* her shoulders relaxed since she was maintaining that altitude above the ground without effort. *Nice updrafts in spite of this early hour.*

Tipping her head to the right, Lanny looked toward Tramway, wanting to keep that main road within reach. Slowly, remembering the camera, she turned to focus away from her direction of flight. Her attention was caught by cursing and a dog's pained bark from somewhere slightly ahead. *Amazing how well sound travels upward.* Her head turned toward the sound. *... the hell is going on?* Lanny stared as she caught sight of motion over the fence of a yard in the block on her right.

"Dammit, let go! No, Max!" A stocky man in a plaid shirt was yanking a corner of a blue tarp whose other end was being pulled by a large black and tan dog. With his free arm the man was ineffectively hitting at the dog with a shovel. *That's an awful thing to do! What a jerk!*

The animal yelped again as a lucky swat connected, but braced and pulled harder, the movement exposing something previously covered by the tarp. It was light-colored against the red brick patio. *Is that what I think it is? A body?*

It was hard to see details since there was now a mound of dirt between Lanny and the object. *...needed brakes to watch longer.* She turned her head once more, hoping for a better view when she saw the man's head swivel to follow the dog's stare. Max had dropped the end of the tarp and was looking directly at her. *OMG!* Gasping, she whipped her head forward, and raised her legs, tilting down to pick up speed as she also tipped toward the mountains again to angle further away from the house. *How can I hide? Not much I can do except hope that guy doesn't worry about me.* Realizing she needed to maintain altitude, she leveled off and the hang glider continued south at its leisurely rate; no amount of wishing would increase its speed.

"Gary, can you hear me, where are you? I think I just saw a dead body, and I'm pretty sure the guy with it saw me. I'm scared spitless."

"Lan, I'm in Tijeras Canyon moving your way as fast as traffic allows. WTF you saying? A dead body? You must be kidding. Can you make the rendezvous point?"

"I'm dead serious and that's not a pun! I'm moving as fast as the wind will let me. Should be enough air to get me there. I'll explain when I'm not flying!"

Lanny stopped talking and concentrated on managing her flight, conserving altitude to make the soccer field.

~~~

"Shit! Max, you pain in the ass! Your barking means I'm screwed. I'm betting that hang glider saw me."

Gordon Jeffers took a deep breath, threw a rock at Max to make him back away from the tarp, and paced another loop around his patio, stopping to pound the back of a chair while circling the furniture, adding to the throbbing headache he had. *Helluva hangover. God, what have I done?* He stared at the lumpy blue tarp so hard it seemed to pulsate and glow. *Gotta get her out of here. Roz, why did you...?* Moving decisively, he opened the door to the garage and lifted the lid on the trunk of the car. *Wish the trunk lip was lower, but on this old beast it's pretty upright.*

Puffing, he dragged the tarp toward the car, Max following as closely as he dared. *Rozlyn sure is heavy for a little bitch! Can't leave her here.* "Ugh!" He grunted and fought her very dead weight into the trunk, closing the lid with quiet finality. *Like Max hasn't already alerted the neighbors.*

Going back to the yard, Jeffers frantically covered the hole he had made, returning a couple of rose bushes to the places they'd occupied in the bed. He tamped the soil furiously. *Max, you're next.*

~~~

Lanny spotted her white van parked on the side street facing the soccer field. She overflew it, turned into the breeze, stalled the wing,

4

and descended gently while she freed her legs and landed as gracefully as she had taken off. A few running steps pacing the wheels, and she stopped as Gary ran to meet her. Her knees almost gave way. She shakily unstrapped and freed herself as he grabbed a wing tip to steady the glider.

"OK, Lan, what the hell are you talking about with this body stuff?"

"Wait a minute 'til I stop shaking. Let's get the glider put away, and I'll tell you what I saw."

She took off her helmet, removed the band holding her auburn pony tail, and shook her hair free, tucking the bothersome strand behind her ear. An environmental lawyer by profession and a birder whenever she had the chance, she honed her ability for accurate observation daily. They sat at a picnic table in the shade. As she swigged water and devoured a protein bar, she explained what she had seen, adding as much detail as she could remember. Her words gave Gary a startling image to absorb.

"There! That's my memory of it. I want to know what I caught with the *Go Pro*. My laptop is in the van. Let's take a look, and now that I feel like me again, I think we ought to go find the place. If that guy really did commit a murder, I want him caught. I need him caught so I can feel safe again!"

Moving to the van, the open door had room for them to be side by side with Gary holding the laptop while Lanny downloaded video info to the computer. She tossed her lightweight shoes in the van and traded them for above the calf boots over her leggings. Zipped the second one and said, "OK, what have we got?"

Playing the images without sound, she fast forwarded the recording until she spotted the action she remembered. The behavior of the man in the short video was at least strange, if not condemning. He was waving a shovel and striking at a large dog seen jumping and dodging the shovel slap while uncovering something nearly white, as the tarp was moved aside. "Poor dog! That SOB was hitting him!" Then the camera shook, making the video blurry. When the picture was clear again, the view was of mountain edge and houses as her head tipped during the flight.

"Not only was he about to bury a body—did you see the hole? He was hurting that dog. We can't do anything about what he's already done, but damn, anyone who'd use a shovel to hit a dog...and I heard it yelp. In fact, that's what first caught my attention," Lanny said, getting angrier as she remembered the vignette she saw while flying.

"I don't know Lanny, it looks suspicious but it's not real clear. Maybe we can see it better when you get it to a bigger screen. You're the one familiar with the law. What do we do now? Who do we tell?"

"We'll talk to the Albuquerque Police soon. Let's find the place first. I want to be sure if something was going on, or maybe I'm wrong about what I saw. I don't want to screw up my credibility."

She let Gary drive and they went north on Tramway while Lanny looked at the video trying to figure out where she was when she saw the event.

"Turn here. I think this street leads far enough into the subdivision to be possible. Now left and let's look closely at houses." They cruised the neighborhood as she tried to spot landmarks.

"It would be easier if I'd been lower, but it felt too close as it was." Lanny peered at the video, and looked up. "Wait, this seems really familiar. I think that's the place on the left in the middle of the block. Color, shape and position are good; can't see over the fence to tell if the back is right."

Gary pulled to the curb in front of the house next door. "Be right back."

"What are you doing? You're out of your mind! What if the guy is there?" She looked up from jotting the address on her computer to see him opening the van door.

"I'll scream and run like hell," he said, laughing as he pushed the door almost closed, and dashed for the side fencing. He used a decorative rock next to it as a stepping stone and peered into the yard.

As she watched him, Lanny slid into the driver's seat and pulled the door closed, preparing for a swift take off, and hoping she wouldn't hear a gunshot. After what seemed like hours, Gary dropped to the ground and hurried back to the van.

"Dammit, don't do that! I don't want to lose a friend over this."

"OK, let's boogie. Yard's empty, but the layout looks like what I saw on the video. Patio with furniture in the right place and there's a flower bed at its edge that looks freshly churned up, with a couple of drooping rose bushes in it."

"When I saw it, the roses were lying on the grass. He's been a busy guy since I flew over. I've got friends in APD. Let's see what they think. I even have one I can call on a Sunday," Lanny said, and the idea of calling Scott Preston caused a shiver of anticipation. Their relationship still had opportunity for non-professional activity.

⁓৶৶⁓

"C'mon Max, in the car!" Jeffers, held the back door open for him, but instead of leaping in the car, with his usual joy at the prospect of a ride, the dog backed away, whining softly.

"Hey boy, it's OK. I'm not going to hurt you. At least not right now." He put as much sugar in his voice as possible, but Max sat and didn't move toward the open door. Jeffers left the car, opened his beer refrigerator and found the box of dog treats Rozlyn stashed there to keep them safe from mice. Grabbing a handful, he stepped to the garage door and tossed one to Max, who instinctively leaped up and caught it effortlessly.

"Ok Max, let's get in the car and go for a ride!" He tossed the remaining treats on the seat, and backed away a couple of steps. Max didn't dash for the car as he normally did, but he finally jumped onto the seat and found the treats while Jeffers slammed the door.

"Sucker, anything for a treat." Jeffers threw himself in the driver's seat, opened the garage, and backed carefully onto the driveway. *No going back, so no sudden moves, nothing out of the ordinary. Just me and the damn dog going for a ride to the hardware store. Yeah, hardware, a shovel for Rozlyn and a bullet for Max. That kind of hardware.*

Max sat on the back seat and whimpered.

Exiting his subdivision, Jeffers headed north on Tramway, then west, passing through Rio Rancho and on to the unpaved portion of roads extending to the edge of the Puerco River valley, hunting for the right combo of empty road and hidden arroyos. *Not so far out that my Cutlass sinks in the sand and can't get back. Not too close to any run down single-wide trailer. That old saying is right. The west mesa is where the bodies are buried. I'm just adding one. Make that two.*

⁓∾⊱⊰∽⁓

Off duty and enjoying it, Scott Preston, "Prez" to everyone except his boss, was in a red tee shirt, red Lobos cap, blue jeans, white athletic socks, feet up on the coffee table with a beer in hand and the baseball game on when the phone rang. He thought about ignoring it. The University of New Mexico Lobos were leading but it was too close since Arizona was known to make surprise comebacks. His innate sense of responsibility took over, and he pulled his cell phone from his jeans pocket. *Lanny? Hmmm, what now? It's been a while. Something serious?*

"Hey, Lanny, what's up? If it isn't critical, or a date, I'm hanging up. Lobos leading by 1 in the bottom of the seventh."

"Prez, I'm still open for us to get together socially, but this is different. I'm sorry to bug you but I think I saw a dead body, and not by natural causes. I want you to see a video I made while flying. Would you be willing to come look and assess what I saw? Do you remember Gary Nesmith? He was helping me with a glider flight and he's still with me. Where can we meet and how soon? I'm way south on Tramway, and if we're right, we should act fast."

Hearing the urgency in her voice, Prez sat up straight, taking his long legs off the table, and with just an instant's thought suggested a place easily accessible to both.

When he arrived at the Flying Star restaurant on Rio Grande, Lanny and Gary were already seated and had ordered lunch. She smiled and waved from the booth when she spotted Preston's lanky figure across the dining space. He pulled Lanny to her feet and wrapped her in a thorough hug. "Obviously, whatever is going on hasn't dampened your appetite. Now what is so crucial you dragged me away from a good game?"

"Hey, fear makes you hungry, and I was starving," Lanny said. "You remember Gary, my flying friend and raging carnivore." Prez reached across the table to shake hands extra firmly. "Hi, You're the guy who helps with the wing." Gary nodded with a mouthful of green chile cheeseburger.

Lanny patted the seat next to her as she scooted over. "Sit beside me and I'll tell you today's story." After the tale unfolded, they watched the video several times, and Preston agreed it might be worth checking out, but not as immediately as Lanny would have liked.

Looking at Gary, Preston said, "No one was home when you looked? Or at least, no one was in the back yard. That's almost trespassing, you know. Lucky he didn't shoot. Maybe he finished planting those roses and was watching a baseball game." He cocked an eyebrow at Lanny as he said the last.

"I know, Prez. I'm sorry to drag you away, but I'm sure something's wrong there. I swear what I saw was more obvious than it seems in the video. I'm going to see how it looks on a bigger screen. Maybe there'll be more definition," Lanny said.

"You do that and let me know. Call it a movie and we can make it a real date. Thanks for the address. I'll make some inquiries via computer, but I think this time your vivid imagination is leading you on, and for now I'm going to see the end of a game," Preston said, patting her hand, then rising to leave.

"Well, I'm going to go with my feeling until proven wrong," Lanny said to his back before he was out of earshot.

She's got good instincts to go with her gorgeous eyes. Dynamite combo —red hair and turquoise eyes. Works well with the other combo—curvy body holding a good brain. Prez enjoyed the walk to his car thinking about another meeting. *Will check and see what's what if only for another meeting.*

~∽∽∽~

Jeffers finally chose a spot that was shielded from casual view by a slope. He leapt out, grabbed the shovel from the back, leaving Max inside with the doors and windows closed. He started digging a burial hole, throwing dirt on the low ridge so if anyone came by he could say he was creating a berm to back drop some tin can target practice. He threw one angry shovelful at the side window of the car, at Max, who was pawing at it, still whining and barking loudly.

"Dammit Max! Shut up! You've always been Rozlyn's dog, not mine, and you'll join her soon enough. Shut up!" He kept excavating shovelful after shovelful until he stood almost waist deep in a trench that angled enough to let him scramble back out.

Before opening the trunk, he climbed the slope near his car and looked in all directions. *Coast's clear. If I have some strength left, this'll soon be finished.* He slid down the bank and popped the trunk. He wrestled the tarp-wrapped body out and onto the ground and rolled her into the trench. *Not as deep as I hoped, but it'll do. Damn, Roz, this was a bad ending.* Max's bed was next, and his food bowls. Then he tossed in a small suitcase filled with medicines, makeup, Roz's purse, and whatever clothes he could cram in.

Max growled as Jeffers opened the front door to get his pistol from under the driver's seat. "Down Max," Jeffers growled back, but as he bent for the gun, Max snarled and jumped on his back and out the door. He bolted away from the car. Jeffers grabbed his gun and snapped off a shot as the dog was disappearing into the sagebrush and weeds. Max yelped in pain and Jeffers smiled. *He won't last long. Coyotes will finish the job. Good riddance!*

The dog's disappearance, instead of death, fueled Jeffers' anger. His adrenalin surge aided the swift filling of the hole. Minutes later he tossed the shovel on the back floor, turned the car and retraced his trail. His tire tracks were still fresh enough for him to be sure he was going back the same way he came. Stories about people getting lost and stuck on the west mesa made him extra cautious. *Don't want to ask for a tow out here. Need nothing to point me to this area. I've never been here since I live way on the other side of town. Right!*

⁓ઊ⁓

A bit depressed by the casual dismissal of the video, Lanny and Gary lingered over their meal after Prez left.

"So Prez wasn't convinced by the video. I know what I saw, and that guy's body language said differently from a casual planting of rose bushes. I wish I had some brilliant idea of what to do next," Lanny said.

"Finish your salad; we need to know who the guy is—that information is easier to see on my computer than a phone, and I have a printer and an idea. Let's go to my place, look up this SOB, and make a plan."

A few minutes later they were on the Bernalillo County website and into the tax records for the house in question, listed along with the surrounding homes.

"Thank God for public records," Gary said as the first sheet was printed, bearing owner's names and addresses.

"Here it is. Gordon Jeffers and spouse Rozlyn are the latest listed owners. There are also listings for the neighbors. What do you think about calling one to see what they know about the Jeffers? You could pretend to be checking for good character as reference for employment," Gary said.

"Good idea. I'll do that chore, and let you go on with your life. You only signed on to assist a flight. This was above and beyond. Sometimes people talk more easily to a woman anyway, so I'll pry gently. Until then, I'm going home, take a tepid bath and try to forget today's stress. Hang gliding is supposed to be fun. Interrupting a murderer isn't on the agenda."

~∾∾∾~

Jeffers pulled into his driveway and looked around. No neighbors were visible on the street. He punched the button on the garage remote and raised the door. As soon as the car was inside he shut the door behind him.

Before leaving the garage, he looked at Rozlyn's small Ford Fiesta dwarfed by his Olds Cutlass Supreme. *Tonight, I lose her car and solidify her visiting out of state relatives. Handy if I had a big lake to drown it in, but leaving it unlocked in the South Valley's "war zone" should be almost as fast since Albuquerque's the stolen car capital of the good ol' U.S.A.! It'll turn into parts, or next stop—Mexico. Hmm, or here's another idea....*

Chapter 2
LATE SUNDAY

Max whined and limped along the packed dirt road, back-tracking slowly in the direction Gordon's car had come. Near one of the turnings they had made, he smelled food—and dogs. He abandoned the route he was taking and hobbled toward a building in the distance. Stopping, he tried to lick the place that hurt so badly but twisting to get at his flank was too painful. He limped onward, hearing dogs barking. He made a small sound totally lost in the frenzied barking of dogs at the fence when he got close. Max collapsed in front of the fenced yard, and lay there as the noise level reached a fever pitch of barks interspersed with a few perfunctory growls.

"Shut up dogs! What has y'all so riled up?" A shirtless man, with black hair pulled back into a low ponytail fastened with white leather strips, shouted at the four frantic dogs as he stepped out the hangar door of a large frame building next to a trailer. He upended his can of Tecate, finished the beer, and threw the empty near the rowdy pack barking at the fence line. The noise of the can hitting the fence startled the dogs into silence, and they bolted from the spot, allowing the owner to see another dog lying outside his property.

"What the hell? Don't I have enough rescue dogs from people dumping 'em out here?" he said as he started for the gate. After he went through and latched it closed, the pack stood at the fence watching the action, occasionally nipping at one another, but now mostly silent.

"Hey, buddy, you just out of steam? Couldn't catch a rabbit?" He knelt down and looked closer. "Holy shit, someone's hurt this poor beggar. Hey fella, it's hard to tell what's the problem with all the blood on you. Take it easy, boy. I'm not going to hurt you. Some bastard already did that, but I'll see what we can do to help. Let me get the pack out of the way, and we'll work on fixing you up."

Whistling to the dogs, he herded them around the trailer and returned alone.

"Easy, boy, I'm Enrique, but I don't know who you are since you aren't dressed with a collar. I'll just call you Buddy for now."

A few minutes later, Max, now Buddy, was lying on the kitchen floor, having collapsed after staggering up the ramp to the door with help from his Good Samaritan. Whines could be heard from the back side of the old single-wide, and Buddy's ears swiveled from those noises to the soothing sounds the man in front of him was making.

"Hmm, hmm, dammmmn, whoooo would dooo something like this?" His tuneless humming accompanied Enrique's gentle hands holding a warm damp rag, sponging off the area, until the source of the blood on his flank was obvious. "Dammmn and dammmn again, you've been shot. I'm not telling you something you don't know, huh? Bleeding's pretty much stopped. Hang on while I step outside to make a call." The dog's eyes closed and his head drooped as Enrique left to stand in the one spot where he got good cell service.

Later, after several phone calls, Enrique reappeared. He knelt down and rubbed Buddy's head, talking as if the dog understood every word, knowing just the soothing sounds were important.

"It would be best to get this treated tonight, but distance to town and costs being what they are and my friend the vet off duty, we'll just make you as comfortable as we can 'til tomorrow morning. Then we'll get you patched up."

Buddy roused enough to eat a few bits of food, drink a big bowl of water, and then went to sleep on an old army blanket under the dining table. Enrique let his sweet yellow lab, Pearl, inside to stop her whining. She sniffed Buddy once, licked his face, curled up along his side, nose to nose, and refused to move. He whimpered in his sleep and growled once, but slept without interruption, curled around the comforting body of his new friend, ignoring the whuffles and complaints from outside.

Chapter 3
MONDAY

E arly in the day Lanny used Bernalillo County tax role information to call the woman who lived next door to Jeffers, hoping she would be home and know what went on in the neighborhood. *Who knew it was so simple to get a lot of info on your neighbors.*

"Good morning, is this Mrs. Smithers? I'm Alice Johnson with Duke City Verification Corporation."

"Good morning. I'm Lois Smithers. Verifying what? What do you want?"

"We are calling about Mr. Gordon Jeffers. He's applied for a job. He listed you as a reference. Do you have a few minutes to talk with me? Or would you rather meet so I can provide identification? I hope you can answer a few simple questions about him."

"You're checking on Gordon's references and I'm one? We're just the next door neighbors, so we don't know much. They haven't lived here long. Came from somewhere in the Midwest, or was it back east somewhere? And we haven't seen a lot of him since he returned from

Afghanistan. I keep saying we. My husband died eight months ago, and he spoke more to Jeffers than I do. He keeps to himself. I think he works at some warehouse, and that's about what I know, but you are welcome to ask questions. Mostly I speak to Rozlyn, his wife, but she hasn't been around for the last few days. At least not when I've been out in the yard. I often see her walking Max, their shepherd-lab-something else, mix. Max is a sweetheart, and she's a nice little woman. She stops to chat and smiles a lot. He's civil, but quiet. Waves when he drives in or out. That kind of thing. That's about all I know."

"Thank you. Perhaps we can finish with a little more information. We are just checking stability and attitude."

"Well, it's not like I'm trying to hear what's going on, but I can't help it when they shout at each other, and so loud that my husband and I could hear her screaming even with our kitchen window closed."

"Hmm, did that happen often?"

"Well, they would get into big arguments with a lot of noise and banging, and then nothing for a while, but the shouting match before this weekend even had Max barking and howling." Mrs. Smithers said.

"Thank you for your honesty, Mrs. Smithers. I don't have more questions. We know that neighbors see things, and don't want to 'tattle.' But we're dealing with important matters and are grateful for your help." With a couple more closing sentences, Lanny hung up and contemplated what she had learned. Repeated violence, at least verbal, had been a situation in Rozlyn Jeffers' life, until this weekend, after which she hadn't been seen.

I think this fits with what I saw, and no wonder she hasn't been seen since the beginning of the weekend. What now, since Prez finds it less than compelling? I'll tell him anyway. More info is valuable... and I'd love to see him again.

At Rio Seco Animal Care, Greg Laird, owner, primary veterinarian, and Enrique's friend since elementary school, spoke softly and ran his hands over Buddy. "This beautiful lab mix is in good shape, except for the bullet wound. He's a good sport about being handled when he's hurting. His teeth are fine, coat's healthy, and he's well fed—obviously a loved pet. That doesn't explain the wound. First thing, since we haven't found an exit wound, we've got to get the bullet out. Well, let's make that second thing. Let's see if what I felt between his shoulders is a chip."

Greg got the scanner and ran it over Buddy's neck and down between his shoulders. The little screen glowed and showed a number and a registry name. "Aha! As I suspected, we've got a winner. Here's the info. Now we'll give your new pal an anesthetic so I can fish for a bullet."

While Buddy was recovering from the anesthesia, Greg carefully put the bullet in a labeled plastic bag with veterinary name, phone, location, and the dog's chip number.

"Ok 'Rique, our next step is to call Bernalillo County Animal Control, and get this to them, since Buddy was shot. They will file an incident report and notify the person on the chip. In the meantime, until he's reclaimed, unless you want him left in the pound, you've got a new boarder."

"Got that right; Buddy's staying with me. I wouldn't let him recuperate or deal with the congestion at the pound no matter how nice the people there are. I'll just take him home." Enrique said.

"Somehow I knew that. You keep being the west mesa's answer to St. Francis. So you end up with all the strays and castoffs. Make more art so you can pay me, OK?"

"Cutting stone as fast as I can in between dog rescues. Greg, call me when you have answers about ownership and who gets to claim this beautiful boy. For now, I'll wrap Buddy up and use him for weight lifting. I can get him in and out of my old Jeep without a problem."

"Do you have a 'collar of shame' his size at home?"

"Yeah, I'll keep the incision protected. You find out where he belongs." Enrique unfolded the blanket he'd used on the trip to the vet, and swaddled Buddy, who was still groggy, 'though his eyes followed Enrique's every move. With Greg holding the door and then opening the back of the Jeep, Enrique carefully got the dog situated.

"Any idea when I'll hear from you?" Enrique asked.

"Nope, it all depends on the County. I'll let you know when I do. The County doesn't move all that fast, might be long as a week or longer. Add another couple of beers to my tab."

～⚬ᘓᘐᘓᘐᘓ⚬～

Jeffers sat with his shoulders hunched over the computer. His fists clenched and he grabbed his thighs until the pain roused him. Between the physical pain and the emotional pain, Jeffers rocked in agony; a tear hit the keyboard. He rubbed his eyes with the back of his hands. *Shit. I'm a crazy drunk, Roz, and you made me so mad, now I am so fucked.*

He took a shuddering breath. *How the fuck do I get out of this? It just gets worse. Stop screwing around asshole and keep checking for glider training companies. No, not gliders, idiot, hang glider training.*

Three companies offered training and flights. OK, *find the guy from Sunday. I'm gonna learn how to fly... and cover my ass.*

～⚬ᘓᘐᘓᘐᘓ⚬～

Lanny thought about the information she gleaned from her phone call, more convinced than ever that Jeffers killed his wife. *An excuse to call Prez and push for more action, 'though I have to admit, we need real evidence.*

Getting his voice mail, Lanny took a deep breath, tried to sound enticing but not too blatant, and plunged into her request.

"Prez, do you have an evening free soon? You mentioned a date, and I've got an offer to make up for interrupting the game. I still want to solve the question of what happened with the guy and dog. We worked well before...."

She put Sunday's event in a closed mental folder until she could work on it, and concentrated on her portion of the suit Carter, King, and Chavez had brought against a local company whose casual dumping of chemicals had killed not only endangered fish in the Rio Grande, but wiped out a family of recently reintroduced River Otter. Those deaths filled her dreams and added fuel to her efforts.

～◌～

Meanwhile, Gordon Jeffers was calling hang glider companies and trying to be casual while gaining info about the person flying on Sunday. The first two companies he called came up empty when he said he was thinking about lessons, but he was hunting for that blue and gray striped wing whose pilot was flying the hang glider so expertly he looked like he might be an instructor. Trying the last one, he found someone who recognized the wing, but said the owner wasn't an instructor, just a local pilot, and they didn't have her name, but he might catch her on a weekend at Sandia Crest, a local launching point for many hang gliding enthusiasts. Jeffers listened with growing impatience to the list of fees, continuing his ruse of interested possible student. Finally, he had his chance to escape.

"Great! That's the information I need. I'll visit the launch site and see what's up."

Her? Jeffers hung up in surprise. "Hell, I never thought about a female pilot. Now I really hope she didn't see me. One mostly accidental killing is enough. I couldn't get that drunk again. The nightmares are godawful. If I could go back...no use thinking...but something will have to happen if old blue and gray can identify me." Talking out loud, he wandered around the empty house, finally ending at the refrigerator, where even staring at a beer didn't raise his spirits.

Chapter 4
THURSDAY

Preston and Lanny finally found overlapping time in their schedules to allow them to meet for dinner. He'd offered to take them out to a restaurant, but Lanny countered with home cooking, and peace and quiet in which to talk about "my case," as she told him when they talked.

He waved a bottle when she opened her door, and said, "Here's a nice wine I haven't tried. If you've got glasses, I've got this for a taste test."

"Come in and I can certainly find glasses," she smiled, and turned to an antique glass-fronted cabinet filled with crystal carafes, bowls, cups and glasses. *God he's good looking she thought as she watched his reflection.* He started opening a bottle of chilled Sauvignon Blanc he brought to go with the fish tacos Lanny mentioned she was making.

"Well, I've got an interesting development to share," Prez said, taking two glasses and pushing his rolled sleeve up with his left hand. Slowing his approach to the wine steward job, he watched her head for the kitchen, her turquoise tee shirt, and black jeans tight enough to be enticing.

"Hold on to that thought. I want to concentrate on what you have, so let me do this first." Rapidly Lanny put bowls of cheese, chopped onion and cilantro, finely sliced cabbage, a pitcher of spicy chipotle drizzling sauce, and a covered holder with warmed corn tortillas on the table. The lightly battered, cubed fish, were in hot oil, turning golden brown.

"OK, I'm ready now."

That innocent double entendre elicited his smile as he handed her a glass, and proffered his for a toast. "Here's to catching bad guys."

"You betcha! I'm for getting one more soon. We just need to figure out how to prove it. Here's to your help." She smiled warmly as they touched rims, and eyes met over their first sip. *Uh huh! That was electric!* Quickly she handed back her glass. *Has he been thinking about me too?* "To the table with this, please." She turned to avoid any further implications for the moment and started draining the fried fish pieces.

Setting down the glasses, Prez responded to her back. "I told you I had a development. Really it's two. First, a notice came in today from Animal Control Department. Early in the week, a west-side vet reported a dog with a gunshot wound. The Control Officer checked its chip on the registry, called, and the number isn't responding. I offered to handle the follow up."

He paused for effect and a sip, grinning. He waited as Lanny turned and was practically dancing, anticipating what he would say next.

"Yeah, come on, come on, tell me what name? You are so mean...if it's not Jeffers, I'll buy dinner next time." Lanny smiled as she choked and spluttered in pretend rage.

"Right you are. Rozlyn Jeffers is the name attached to the dog at the registry. And, since you can confirm it, the dog's name is Max. Pretty good tie together for me. Now for the second one. Jeffers was arrested on a simple assault charge last year for a problem at a bar. So we know he isn't reluctant to use his fists."

She slapped her hot pad on the counter. "I knew it! Missing woman, and her dog shot, and not accidentally. And as you can see, dinner's ready if you'll put the guac on the table. Biscochitos for dessert. Maybe not totally New Mexican, but a good southwestern dinner."

While they piled fillings on the tortillas, she told him about looking on the tax rolls and her call to Mrs. Smithers on Monday, sharing the unguarded information told her by the neighbor.

"I'm not thrilled with the way you went about getting that information, but let's enumerate it. We've got more than one loud argument, suspicious activity in the yard, and a woman who usually walks their dog—who hasn't been visible since the weekend." Prez took a breath, held up the bottle with a questioning look, and poured both Lanny and himself a second glass.

"Plus the wounded dog and the unanswered phone," Lanny added. "And it appears things were rough, at least loud, with a guy who beats on people. This weekend, perhaps things changed in the Jeffers house. Now we need to find out where she is. Or...if...she is!"

Comfortably seated near one another on the couch, their talk continued about other things over the cookies and coffee. Lanny encouraged Prez to stay until he was sure the wine buzz was gone, and for them to formulate some sort of plan since both had work commitments Friday. Preston was convinced Jeffers was going nowhere since nothing had been done to alert him to the possibility of legal pursuit. He took on the task of talking with the veterinarian.

In spite of Prez's concerns about the honesty of the action, Lanny would call Mrs. Smithers again and see if Rozlyn worked, and if so, where? They wrapped up a companionable evening that had gotten late while they discussed things other than crime.

Refusing his offer to help with dishes, Lanny opened the door for Prez to leave. He bent down and kissed her cheek, then hugged her tightly and whispered "sweet dreams" in her ear. Grinning as he turned her loose, she pulled his head down and added a kiss on his lips, which he heartily returned.

"Now I have something to dream on too," Prez said as he departed, leaving Lanny dreaming about parts unseen.

Chapter 5
FRIDAY

After parking the car, Jeffers stood at the Fiesta's back end, waiting for the shuttle driver to pick him up. He held the handle on a small rolling suitcase, and tried to feel casual about his presence in the city's airport parking lot. *I'm just another citizen on a short vacation. Or maybe I'm going on a business trip overnight. That's it, and why I don't look excited. But getting rid of Roz's car is pretty exciting.* The driver took Jeffers suitcase and added it to the pile in the back of the van.

"Which airline?" he was asked as he climbed aboard.

"Uh, Southwest," responded Jeffers, shaken, as memories flooded back. He remembered when he'd taken Roz to Cancun. Their vacation was idyllic, even with the mild sunburn he got. He felt again the gentle touch of her hand as she rubbed aloe gel on his shoulders. He shuddered to erase the fingers on his back. *No more drinking, no more! No way to explain it was an accident, but drinking made it worse.*

He leaned back on the seat, closed his eyes and waited for the van to stop. "Southwest," the driver said, and Jeffers let the other two passengers off first. He exited the shuttle, retrieved his suitcase, and handed the driver a dollar.

He walked into the main terminal, turned left, and went down the escalator to baggage claim. He was relieved it seemed to be in between landings and there were very few people around. He sauntered into the empty men's restroom, entering the stall furthest from the door. He pushed the suitcase into the back corner and wiped the handle, flushed for effect in case anyone had come in, and exited the still empty men's room.

Texting Uber, he requested a ride and sat on an empty bench until his driver arrived. Giving him an address several blocks from his home, Jeffers rode in silence, watching the mountains and thinking about his next move. He gave the driver a small tip and let the car drive off as he turned toward the house. After the car was out of sight around the corner, he changed direction and walked up the street, then another block before turning around a corner to his home. *Well, that should keep 'em looking elsewhere.*

Chapter 6
SATURDAY

In the early morning, near the tram station on Sandia Crest, Jeffers walked up and stood watching with several others as volunteers with the Land of Enchantment Hang Glider Association helped members launching from the ramp. They had an information table with a young girl answering questions.

Waiting at the back of the casual line, Jeffers guessed as young as the girl looked, she was probably in high school. He tried not to stare as she handed out flyers and pointed to various members of the club for information when she didn't have the answer. His turn finally came and he stepped up and spoke in answer to her inquiring look and "how can I help you?"

"I was taking pictures last Sunday, and I got a dramatic picture of a beautiful blue and gray hang glider against the Sandias. I'd like to send it to the pilot, but I don't know who it is. Do you know who owns it?"

"Oh, that must be Lanny. She flies from here with us. Wide diagonal stripes? Blue and gray with white accents?" Jeffers nodded, afraid to trust his voice. "Let me see if her phone number is here on my list."

"Would you have her address too? That way I can just send it to her." Jeffers gave her his friendliest smile, stepped back a step and looked at the launch area as if not really concerned.

"Here you go. I'm sure she'll appreciate the picture." The young woman handed Jeffers a piece of paper with a name and information on it, which he casually tucked in a pocket.

"Thank you," he smiled warmly and it was truly felt, but not for the expected reason. Jeffers moved over to watch a launch, and then trailed after a group leaving the area. He stopped at the edge of the parking lot and bent over clutching his stomach. Trying to breathe and stop his heart from pounding, he felt nauseous. *Got it! I'll stay a free man. Woman has to have an accident—with her hang glider or another way. I'm trapped in this. Can't believe she didn't see me. So she goes.*

He slouched in the driver's seat of his dark blue Cutlass, took out the note and read, Lansford Mitchell, Lanny, 1540 Vista Marquez, ABQ, 425-2244. *Jackpot, of sorts. I want another way out. Leave the country? I could be in Mexico in a few hours. Then what? Survive how? I have to stay here.*

⌒⌒⌒

The registry company for Max's chip had the veterinarian's office numbers. Prez called Greg Laird to find out what had happened to the dog. Greg had Enrique's number on his phone and shared the contact so APD had all his information. The detective's next step was phoning Enrique Garcia to locate Max and take possession of the animal. Enrique understood Max might be evidence in a case, not of just animal abuse, but murder.

Jeffers was startled to see a uniform at his door. *What the hell? It's OK, I'm just home alone for a week or two. Remember my story. Tell myself again.* When he opened the door, before he started to speak, the policeman identified himself as an APD Officer, presenting his badge and introducing himself as Julian Martinez.

"Is Mrs. Rozlyn Jeffers at home?"

Jeffers reminded himself he had no reason to be concerned, everything was going well, but his heart was thudding as he spoke. "No, she isn't, sir. What can I help you with? I'm her husband. Has she done something illegal?" He stopped to clear his throat.

"No, but a dog, name of Max, was found with a gunshot wound, and he was chipped. The chip information says he belongs here. The phone number is listed as belonging to Rozlyn Jeffers." The officer waited for Jeffers to respond.

"I, we don't have a dog. Well, we did, but he ran away, and we put notices in the local neighborhood email group, and nobody ever returned him...that was a while back." Jeffers stammered a bit and stopped.

When the silence threatened to become awkward, Martinez continued.

"We've tried calling the number, but there is no answer. When this happens, our next step is to contact the owner personally. You say she's not here. Will she be back soon?"

"Well, she's out of town visiting her folks and some friends in South Texas. They were all going to some place they like in Mexico. Her cell phone doesn't work internationally, so I can't contact her. I don't enjoy Mexico as much as she does. I just let her go with her folks. We don't own that dog anymore. I don't know why her number was still on that chip," Jeffers said in a rush.

"It happens more often than you'd think. People just forget to change the number or the address. I'm sorry to have bothered you. The dog must have gotten away from its new owners. As soon as you hear from her, please have her call, so we can clear up this confusion. Here's my card."

Jeffers looked at the card and then the policeman, and slowly, after reading it, said, "I certainly will, Officer Martinez. It should be within a day or so. They weren't going to spend long across the border."

The officer walked to his patrol car and drove off. Then Martinez contacted Preston as planned. "Sir, Ms. Jeffers was not at home, and Mr. Jeffers said they don't have a dog anymore. He said he didn't know why her number was still associated with a chipped animal. I told him it was probably just not changed and left."

"Thanks, Martinez. Good job keeping it simple not challenging him on the dog. We're trying not to spook Jeffers before we have all the evidence we need to arrest him and make sure the charges are air tight."

Preston called Lanny soon after.

"I've made an appointment to go see a man, out on the west mesa, about a dog tomorrow afternoon. Its name is Max. Would you like to come along for the ride? And you have a leash and collar?" His chuckle let her know he recognized she could not bear to miss this piece of the puzzle.

"Of course! What time? I'll bring Topper's old collar and leash. I knew saving those was a good idea, even if I couldn't face having another dog yet."

Prez responded. "Come here about two. We'll leave your car, and take my Subaru. No sense sticking two vehicles in the sand."

Chapter 7
SUNDAY

Lanny's bungalow was a solid concrete construction dating from World War Two, with a narrow driveway running alongside the house to a separate garage at the back of the property. When this house was built, one car was a luxury. There were no two car families in this modest neighborhood. Her narrow drive was matched by the size of the garage. Just enough room for her nine-year old Toyota Camry and a person squeezing in and out. The limited space in front held camping gear on shelves, and skis hung from beams by bungee cords. Lanny's white van and beloved hang glider were under cover in a storage unit several blocks away.

She was writing notes on the pollution case that had become a large, complex issue and missed Saturday's flight. Wanting to visit with flying friends, she left home shortly after eleven to join the Hang Glider Association members for Sunday noon lunch at Quarter Celtic, their standard meeting place. They liked the patio—and the award-winning house beers.

Lanny had finished eating and ended her part in a conversation at her table. She was walking past the rest of the group on her way out, when Gina, a new teen volunteer who hoped to earn flight lessons by handling things at the launch site, grabbed her sleeve. "Hey, Lanny, did that photographer get in touch with you?"

"What photographer are you talking about?" Lanny crouched down near Gina's seat to be eye to eye.

"The guy who took a photo of you a couple of Sundays ago. He said he had a great shot of your wing against the mountain and wanted to send it to you, so I gave him your address and phone number." Seeing the strained look on Lanny's face, Gina continued, "I hope that was OK."

Mustering a smile as she stood up, Lanny replied, "Well, I'd rather not have personal information given out, so I was just surprised. Did you happen to get his name?" Gina shook her head.

"No worries; I'm sure he'll be in touch to send it." Lanny waved a hand in dismissal and resumed her departure, trying to look casual rather than showing how unnerved she felt. Sitting in the dim underground parking lot, she hugged herself to stop her violent shaking. *Ok, take a deep breath, you can't drive like this.* Breathing carefully, she regained some of her composure but the knowledge of her vulnerability remained.

Checking the time, Lanny drove directly to meet Prez at his place. She had been happily anticipating the visit to the west mesa to see the guy holding Max, but now she found she was trembling with nerves. *Prez'll help. I can tell him and know he'll understand.*

He was waiting when she pulled up to the curb, and after a shaky hello, her tight hug made him look questioningly at her. "What's going on? Tell me while we move."

"I'm busted, and scared! A kid with the hang gliding group unthinkingly gave someone my name and number!" She shared her fears from the news she had just received, and they discussed the probability of the photographer being Jeffers.

Lanny's voice sounded shrill in her ears. "It's too big a coincidence. No one, except friends I have enlisted for the job, has ever provided pictures of my flying. Knowing Jeffers has my address scares me. I'm sure he knows I saw him."

"OK, you're safe with me, away from home, and we'll work that problem after we—if we—get any help from Max to find the answer to what the dog was doing on the west mesa." Prez glanced at Lanny, and saw her furrowed brow and white-knuckled, intertwined fingers. He patted her knee, and rested his hand there when she covered it with her own. *Even this small contact helps. Breathe slowly.*

Lanny gave him a strained smile and took a deep breath, "I just hope we find something soon to tie him to our missing person and the lump on the patio...." Regaining her balance, and with directions in hand, Lanny navigated while Prez drove.

～ﬡﬡ～

Jeffers woke late. "Fuck it, what a headache. Yeah, idiot, what do you expect when you kill a six-pack and follow it with the last of the cheap tequila?" Berating himself didn't make his head hurt less. He took a lengthy shower, then made some strong coffee and washed down several aspirin with his second cup. *Holy shit! When will I learn?*

Because of his late start, Jeffers didn't get to Lanny's house 'til after noon on Sunday. Noting the layout, he parked his Cutlass on the other side of the street at the end of the block. That location gave him a good view of the driveway. Jeffers settled in to wait. *How will I know if she is the right person? Damned distant—the view was brief. Somehow I'll know.*

Four hours later, tired of moving his car, circling the block, and finding inconspicuous places to watch from with no action at her home, and neighbors watering lawns or lounging in their yards, he decided to leave. He drove around yet another block and parked to think about his next action. Wanting something to eat to chase away his acid stomach, and a chance to take a piss, reinforced his decision to chuck it temporarily. *I'll know she's home when I see lights on.*

❧❧❧

It was a lengthy drive, but with only a couple of wrong turns, they found Enrique's place as arranged. The bulk of the canine pack had been put in the back, so the only dogs barking at the fence were Pearl and Max, still wearing the plastic cone.

"Actually, I think Mr. Garcia is going to be glad to have us take Max. There have been some issues between Max and a couple of the other dogs he has rescued. He mentioned that shuffling them around to keep them separated has been a hassle," Prez said as he got out of the car.

"They act like an alarm system," Enrique said, approaching them from his sculpting workshop. "OK kids, behave. Pearl, sit."

Prez spoke first as he dug in his back pocket, retrieved his credentials and showed them to Enrique. "I'm Detective Scott Preston with the APD, and this is Lanny Mitchell, who saw Max before the shooting incident. I am betting that is Max with the cone and the limp, and you must be Enrique Garcia. As I said when we made this appointment, Mr. Garcia, I got your name and number from the report sent in about a dog in a shooting incident. We want to confirm Max is the animal Lanny saw."

"Sir, you're right on both counts. I'm Enrique Garcia; I seem to be the St. Francis of the west mesa. Lost and injured dogs keep ending up on my doorstep. Buddy, I mean Max, is a good example of that. He arrived without a name, and the blood loss from the shooting had him worn out. He's that gorgeous, only slightly limping, Shepherd, Lab mix. He has healed fast. The Yellow Lab is Pearl, keeping him company. My other rescues are in the back since a couple of them have decided to take offense at the newcomer." He held out his hand to shake. Prez responded with a smile, "Thanks for taking care of our witness."

Enrique turned to the dogs, "Here Max, let me get that cone off you. He really doesn't need it any longer and I should have taken it off earlier today." Relieved to get rid of the cone, Max vigorously shook all over, and then enthusiastically pushed Pearl nearly off her feet.

"Max, Max, come here boy." Lanny knelt, and Max limped up to her, his tail wagging furiously. "Hi Max boy, how are you feeling?" She put out a hand, for him to sniff, then wrapped him in a hug, as he nearly pushed her over, with affection and a need to be close. "You've been well taken care of, but you really miss your mom, don't you?" The big black and gold lab mix soaked her cheek with licks, while he wiggled and made happy mutterings.

Turning from Enrique, where he had been learning details about Max's story, Prez looked at Lanny. "Now that you have a new BFF, let's see what he knows and how he can help us...and Rozlyn. Mr. Garcia, this dog is probably a witness to a murder, and will need to come with us for protection as he can identify the suspect."

Enrique said, as he looked at Max, "When you called, I thought he would probably end up going with you. He's been the perfect house guest. I think Pearl will miss him, but the pack in the back yard won't!"

Lanny pulled the collar and leash from her jean's pocket and held them for Max to sniff. He held still while she fastened the collar, and then tugged on the leash the moment it was attached. He whimpered at the gate, and yanked her outside when she opened it.

"Enrique, thanks for the care you gave this dog! It was nice to meet you. I guess we're going now!" She was laughing at her abrupt departure, but then it became serious as he dragged her down the road, away from their parked car. "Max—stop. Wait a minute! Sit!" Catching her breath, she called back. "Prez, he has something he wants to do! You'll bring the car? Or walk with me? Better make it the car! We're on a mission. OK boy."

Max whined again and barked once, but kept pulling, so Lanny gave him length on the leash and let him lead her at a very swift walk. He hobbled but wouldn't slow down. There were twists and turns on the dusty car tracks cutting through the brush, and at several, Max started one way and backtracked before forging onward. He was accepting but distracted when Lanny stopped him and offered a drink from her water bottle. Although his limp was worse, when Lanny tried to stop him, he insisted on going forward.

She guessed they were over a mile from Enrique's house, with Prez slowly following in his SUV, when Max stopped. He sat and whined. Lanny saw the disturbed soil in front of her and motioned for Prez to stop before he got too close.

He killed the engine and walked in the middle of the dusty trail, looking at the edges as he joined them.

As he got near, Lanny said, "I must be imagining the odor, but I thought when we first got close...." She stopped, and patted Max's head. "I'm sorry boy. You know, don't you? Prez, you ready to call and get a team out here? I'm afraid we've found Rozlyn."

"No argument from me. Max's behavior says more than words could. His favorite person is here alright. He's done a great job for her. I'll call in for a field investigator and violent crimes detective. Will also send the GPS coordinates while you keep Max away from the site. We've got to identify this place so we don't lose it. Walk carefully, there might still be tire tracks to mark. I hope for our sake it doesn't take long for all to arrive."

While Prez made calls, Lanny kept hold of the leash, and finally giving up pulling on it, Max lay in the middle of the road, his head on his paws.

After stopping to pick up dog supplies, it was late in the evening before Prez, Lanny, and their new friend Max, pulled into the driveway at his house. "Alright Max, we're home," he said to the dog sitting upright on the back seat. Max leaned forward and licked Prez's ear, then stood on the seat waiting to get out. "Whew, you're not a lightweight are you?" he grunted as he lifted Max down, protecting the dog's back leg.

Laughing, Lanny caught up with the two of them at the front door. She was carrying a bag of Iams dog food and box of Milk Bone treats for large dogs. "OK boys, let's get Max settled. Good of you to keep this evidence alive. We know he's safe here and your place sure beats having him way out on the mesa."

Prez rubbed Max's head and responded. "Well, he's a good companion and he's faring better than we are. You and I missed at least one meal waiting for the crime boys to get to us. I'm glad it's over to them. That Max's bed and bowls were found in the grave was the least tragic part of this. They've been kept as evidence, so Max will end up on an old blanket tonight. But back to the living. We need food. Stay with me and have a sandwich? There's either toasted cheese or peanut butter. What wine goes with peanut butter? Or a beer? Perhaps not gourmet, but the starving can't be too particular."

Laughing, Lanny assumed a haughty tone and accent. "Oh, I think a light white, perhaps a Pinot Grigio will pair well with PB and J. Just tell me where to find a knife; I make a gourmet sandwich."

Lanny set down a dish filled with dog food and another filled with water while Prez was still talking and checking the fridge for strawberry jam to go with the peanut butter he'd found in the pantry. Max wagged his tail and crunched kibble. After a lengthy drink, his drippy muzzle sprayed water as his head swiveled from Prez to Lanny.

Lanny coated bread with peanut butter and strawberry jam as Prez filled glasses with wine and added a second placemat to the table. He pulled out a chair for Lanny as she brought plates and then circled to his seat on the other side of the table. "It's not the happiest reason for a toast, but today has to be counted a success since we are closing in on finishing this tragedy. Salud Lanny, and here's to a swift completion of this case."

Gently clinking her glass rim to his, she added, "Here's to Rozlyn's peaceful sleep, and Max's help."

Hearing his name, Max sat up and rested his head on Prez's leg. Rubbing his head, Prez said, "This good boy has distracted us from our bigger current problem. What is Jeffers up to? When we tie him to the body we found, we'll bring him in, but until then, I'm going to ask someone on patrol to cruise your area just for safety's sake. I'll expect you to let me know you're home and inside securely... unless you want to stay here."

Lanny smiled at Prez. "Thanks, nice invitation, but I'll take a raincheck. Tonight my own bed—I'll let you know I'm safely inside. And a second thanks; I'll sleep easier knowing the area has been checked."

Prez walked Lanny to her car. She stopped before crossing to the driver's side to thank him for the day, but he took her hand and gently pulled her toward him for a good night hug and lengthy kiss which she leaned into with pleasure.

"I'll add that to the good things about today. It helps the balance. I'll call when I get home."

Chapter 8
SUNDAY NIGHT

Jeffers sat in his darkened Cutlass and watched from a block away as a patrol car made a second circuit of Lanny's street. *Something going on? Not a good idea to get near her place now. No lights yet anyhow. It'll have to wait.* Jeffers decided to give up for the night. When the police car was out of sight, he drove in the opposite direction. Worrying, he slowly made his way home.

"Lights! I want lights." He spoke aloud as he rushed to flip switches in the kitchen, dining, and living rooms. Jeffers went to the kitchen where he buttered a stale piece of bread and ate it as he walked to and fro. He punched a door as he walked past. *How am I going to get out of this? Who'd believe it was a fucking accident? I should have walked out, away, anything but hit her! I've got to get lost or get rid of that witness somehow.* His commitment to sobriety faded with nervousness. The sound of ice hitting glass was comforting, but not as much as the warmth of alcohol sliding into his stomach and spreading throughout his body. He wished Lanny would just disappear without his having to make that happen. He again drank enough to have the room and bed whirling as he faded out.

He was being chased through an unknown building, climbing stairs with no handrails, running through passages that were claustrophobically narrow or dark or so expansive no orientation was possible. He bumped into walls he hadn't seen, fell over invisible obstacles on the floor, and slammed his head into a low-hanging sign. He tried without success to make out its words in the dark. Interrupting this restless night's sleep, his alarm roused him. Sweating and breathing hard, he wiped his face with the edge of the sheet. *Jeez, head hurts! Can I make it to work? Got to keep it all regular. Noise in warehouse may finish me off. Coffee essential.* Jeffers staggered to the kitchen, started the coffee maker, found the bathroom, and vomited before a long hot, then cold, shower helped revive him.

Chapter 9
MONDAY

Sitting in her office, Lanny had opened a brown bag lunch and spread out her salad, sourdough bread, and cheese, when her phone dinged. It announced a text message from Prez. *Call.*

Calling and hearing his voice at the other end were almost instantaneous.

"Prez, what good timing. I've just gotten back from court and am having lunch at my desk. As I said, when I got home, all was quiet there. How's Max? What's going on?"

"Lanny! How's your day? Glad those drive bys found nothing and were reassuring. You're valuable to this case, among other things."

She grinned, hearing the smile in his voice with that comment. *Day dreams will have to wait for later.*

The silence was brief before Prez continued, "I thought you'd want to know, APD had Jeffers' prints from his old arrest and they're are on many of the items in the cache of articles found with what we are assuming is Rozlyn's body. Those things were hers, based on purse contents, but we have to be positive. We should know that for certain later today. I've asked for a rush on a body ID to accompany Jeffers' fingerprints."

She heard him rustling papers. "Max seems fine. He's a quiet lump lying here at my desk. Special treatment today, but this won't continue. He's lots better. Limp is almost nonexistent. Healthy boy who's healing fast."

Lanny paused before she spoke. "Even though I expect it, knowing he'll go away is tough. What's going to happen to Max?"

"Dunno yet. He'll go to a foster family until relations can be contacted when the case is settled, unless Jeffers is innocent—which I doubt. But I've got more info to add to this case. Late last week a suitcase was found in the men's room at the Sunport. Some idiot saw it behind a toilet, and instead of calling the authorities in case it was explosive, he opened it. Hoping for jewels, drugs, who knows? Anyhow, when it didn't have anything valuable, so he says, he dragged it to a ticketing agent and told her where he found it." As Prez took a breath, Lanny leaped in.

"OMG, it has to be Rozlyn's or you wouldn't be telling me." She heard Prez's impatient fingers drumming on his desk. "OK, I'll stop jumping ahead. Finish the story."

"Yeah, it's probably Rozlyn's. The fingerprints on the outside weren't Jeffers. They turned out to be from our stupid Samaritan or thief wannabee. But, on the inside, Jeffers' prints are all over it. Why a suitcase there? Was he going to leave and changed his mind? This guy doesn't seem to be the brightest bulb, so what was he thinking? The clothes stuffed in there are all female apparel, so he hadn't packed for himself, and by then she was already dead, so what the hell? Why was he at the Sunport?"

The silence lingered as Lanny mused on possibilities.

"I've got nothing that makes sense, and there's no need for us to keep wondering without more info. We should talk later," Prez said.

"Sounds good. Is tonight too soon? I'd like to see Max again before he goes elsewhere. I can pick up a pizza. What kind do you like? There's a Dion's on the way to your place."

Chapter 10
MONDAY EVENING

Pizza eaten and Max lying at their feet, satisfied with all the hugs and petting he got from Lanny, they spent the rest of the evening curled up on the couch, talking briefly about the suitcase, the next steps, and then chatting about anything that interested them.

Lanny shared a brief rant about what was going on at the attorney's office where she was dealing with men who too often discounted her ideas. Prez hugged her tighter and listened sympathetically while he enjoyed the subtle lavender aroma in her hair.

Before leaving, Lanny offered to keep Max since it would be easier for her. Dogs often came with their owners to her office. She also realized, being honest with herself, she was still missing Topper, her German Shepherd. Prez was grateful since it was difficult for Max to be with him at Homicide.

In one of those flukes of timing, Lanny and Max arrived at her place, and got settled inside during one of Jeffers' absences from his watching post.

He saw lights on when he drove down her street to park at the corner. *When the lights go out there'll be a chance. Think there's going to be an accident in this old house.*

Jeffers used the mottled darkness of large trees and the added blackness underneath to quietly steal to the back door where he slipped a wedge under the plastic-paneled storm door. *It'll take time to break that open. Maybe she'll panic.* Then he tiptoed to the front where he left a rag he'd soaked in paint thinner at the door jamb joint, with a burning cigarette tucked in a match pack near it. *That'll do it. Got to get to car and get out of here. Move!*

He was in his car and around the corner before the spark caught and matches flared. The rag burst into flame, singeing the paint on the door. In seconds the old paint flashed and the fire licked up the side of the door. Decades-old paint and wood older still were an ideal combustion combination. The front of the house was ablaze in minutes, with flames spreading across the door and over the siding.

Max's frantic barks were strident! Sleepily she shook herself awake, unaccustomed now to a dog's voice in her home. She threw on her robe as she ran toward the front door to see what had Max so upset. She smelled smoke before she saw flickering light through the blinds on the front windows.

"911! Gotta call! Fire?! Where—where's my phone? Good boy, Max, come with me." Lanny dashed back toward her bedroom while hollering. She grabbed her phone from the table next to her bed and punched 911.

"Help! My house is on fire! My dog and I are getting out the back, but I need help fast."

The dispatcher took her address and told Lanny she had contacted the closest fire station, and for her to stay on the phone and get out swiftly.

Dropping the phone on the bed, she threw on jeans, a tee shirt, slipped on a pair of cowboy boots, picked up her phone, slung her purse over her shoulder and ran to the dining room. There she grabbed her laptop and the thick file of court papers she'd been working on, and the file containing her personal papers from the bottom drawer of her desk. Juggling those, she caught the leash from the back of the chair nearest the utility room and kept moving toward the door. The voice of the operator, small in her hand, wanted to know if she was out of the house. "Not yet, but we are close."

Hurrying through the utility room to the back, she opened the door, unlocked the screen door with the storm insert, and pushed. The door didn't budge. She dropped the things in her hands on the adjacent dryer and shook the screen door with both hands. "Shit! The door won't open." *Stubborn and stuck. Now? OK, no time to mess around.* She leaned back, braced herself against the dryer, raised one knee to her chest and gave a vicious kick to the door, nearly falling as it gave way. The operator was saying, try again, as Lanny ignored her to knock the screen insert loose and kick part of the panel out of the way. The frame didn't open, but the nylon screening was already ripped and she pulled it away with little effort. "Got it, we're about out."

She grabbed her things and stepped through the large hole she'd created. "Come on Max. Come here boy!"

Lanny patted her hip with her mostly empty hand and whistled encouragingly. After a moment's hesitation, Max sailed over the remnant of the kick panel on the bottom, yelping with pain when he landed on his sore leg. She rubbed his head and fastened the leash to his collar, "I'm sorry that hurt, but good boy. Let's get out of here." She coughed as smoke from the front yard caught her. She told the operator, "I'm hanging up now. Thanks for staying with us. I hear sirens." She stuck the phone in her back pocket and headed diagonally through the neighbor's yard.

She was debating about waking the neighbors when sirens on trucks racing down the street did it instead. Controlled chaos overwhelmed her, and had Max barking furiously, as fire engines screamed to a stop in front of her house. Neighbors up and down the street appeared in various kinds of sleeping attire. Police sirens added to the cacophony as they arrived following the 911 call. Water shot from hoses, officers shouted at people to stay back, Max kept barking and pulling on his leash. Lanny collapsed on the next door neighbor's steps, watching the scene in disbelief. Frances, the widow who lived in the house, sat with her and wrapped an arm over her shoulders. Later she brought a cup of coffee, a lightweight shawl, and a shopping bag to hold the armload of papers Lanny clutched. She gave Frances a shaky smile. "Thanks, my teeth were chattering."

In the midst of the apparent confusion, the firefighters efficiently got the flames beaten down and soaked the roof to be sure the fire was doused. Several hours passed and it was nearly dawn before calm returned.

"You were lucky we have a substation so close, ma'am," the captain said to Lanny as the members of his team were rolling up hoses and packing away equipment. "The other thing saving your house was calling as soon as you did."

"If it hadn't been for Max...," Lanny replied, patting the dog's head as he leaned contentedly against her leg. She swallowed hard, tearing up, as she thought about another outcome. The officer patted her shoulder and she realized it was light enough to see as she smiled at his sympathy.

She looked back at her house and the captain turned to check on the progress by his firefighters. Neither of them noticed a dark blue Cutlass cruise by in line with several other cars. The fire team was nearly done, so the Captain gave her a casual two finger salute, and said, "We're about to leave and glad it wasn't any worse. Now you get to do repairs."

Lanny nodded distractedly as Max growled and tugged hard on his leash. "No, Max, come on let's see how bad it is." He whined, but trotted with her as she slogged across the yard to her house. The front was well scorched and the eaves and roof in front were burned, but since behind the siding veneer the house was cement, no significant damage occurred. *Thank God for that concrete-solid construction.* The front door was still locked and although it would have to be replaced, it was secure for the moment.

Walking around the house and stopping at the back, Lanny set down the bag holding her rescued belongings. She pulled on the screen door. When it still didn't open, she looked more closely and saw something at the bottom corner.

"What the hell?" She started to kick the block sideways, but thought better of it. *This could also be evidence.* She used her phone for a couple of shots. She checked her photos. One too bright with the flash, but the other was adequate. *Not a contest winner, but it shows what I need.* Then she pried the object loose with a foot. Picking it up with a bandana from her pocket, Lanny recognized an industrial black rubber doorstop. She dropped it in the bag, opened the door, walked through the interior, realizing what could have been, and was grateful once more for Max. Starting to unclip his leash, she knelt down and hugged him and leaned her head on his. Max licked her ear and cheek in return and that sweet action triggered the tears. Sagging to the floor, Lanny sobbed violently, her body wrenching with each gasp. Tears poured down her cheeks and onto her tee shirt. After several minutes, while she petted Max and sniffled, calming both of them down, she took a shuddering, deep breath and shakily stood up. "I'm OK Max. We can handle this. How about some breakfast, big boy? You've earned a steak, but this will have to do for now. You were wonderful Max! Saved our lives and my home."

She burned off nervous energy talking while adding more kibble to his empty bowl. Fresh water was next, and then she turned her attention to the house as she peeled the plastic wrapper off a protein bar.

The smoke odor was strong but bearable. She went through the place opening windows. She turned on the swamp cooler and immediately turned it off since it pulled in the smoke odor from the roof.

"Nearly 7 a.m. APD and Prez need to know what's happened. I think an arson investigator is in order."

Chapter 11
TUESDAY MORNING

Jeffers pounded the steering wheel. "Fuck, fuck, and double fuck! That woman with the fireman had to be the pilot. And next to her was Max! I'm sure of it. Of all the bad luck! Where was a coyote when I needed one? They have to know now, since she's got Max, that was no typo on his chip. I'm toast. Get out of town now! I wish these bloody cars would get out of my way." Driving frantically, but without much thought, he got to Central, turned right and headed west.

On the outskirts of Albuquerque, he realized gas was critically low. The busy crowd at Love's truck stop on I-40 paid no attention to Jeffers as he filled the tank, grabbed a bottle of water, a package of jerky, paid with his credit card, and left, still headed west.

"Where can I hide? Roz, if I could go back, I wouldn't have hit you so hard. Hell, now, I wouldn't have hit you at all! I...I guess it's going to be Mexico even if it's not my first choice."

※

"Prez, what do you mean, he's gone? Gone how? Where?" To her own ears, Lanny knew her voice sounded whiny and strained. Knowing she sounded weak made her angrier, but she couldn't help it. Awareness that Jeffers was probably responsible for the arson attempt made her jumpy. "How the hell was he not arrested? The guy left evidence all over the place. You've got a body. I've sworn to what I saw, and you have the video. All that ought to mean something."

"Easy Lanny, it seems worse than it is. We agree it's time to arrest him. There's already enough to hold him, and I'm sure there will be something to tie him to your arson. We'll find Jeffers and bring him in. You won't have to worry," Prez said, taking a quick breath and continuing before Lanny could rant again.

"When the APD went to his house, intending to make an arrest, no one was home. The garage was empty. The Ford Fiesta is missing so it is out there somewhere, but we're betting he's in his Cutlass. He's not at the warehouse. He didn't go in to work this morning. So now there is an APB out on him. With an All Points Bulletin, he won't be loose long. Relax, Lanny, you've got Max. Talk about an early warning system...."

"I know. He's at my side. I brought him to the office with me. With the mess at home, I didn't want to leave him in the yard. I've been busy with calls. Insurance, handymen, roofers, tree guy. And getting ready for the case postponed to the end of the week. He's been patient. Just lying here, being a good contented guy, aren't you Max?" The dog's ears perked at his name, he looked at Lanny and his tail tip flipped a couple of times, then his eyes closed again.

~∽∾∽~

Jeffers was alert for New Mexico State Police cars. He stayed in the right lane, sandwiched between a couple of eighteen wheelers. As usual, I-40 was full of those giant semis. He felt small and inconspicuous in comparison. *What the hell, drove 40 to Arizona once, but never got off the highway. No time like the present. Find a major road and head south.* Two State Police cars went by the other way, heading toward Albuquerque. Suddenly Jeffers knew his car was flashing neon red instead of nondescript dark blue.

"I'll take the first road south. I need to get off this. Too few exits." He found minor reassurance in hearing his own voice. It felt as if someone else was giving him guidance.

Nearing Grants, he saw the sign for New Mexico Highway 117 and El Malpais National Monument. Although Jeffers had heard about those lava fields, other than the outcrops next to the highway, he'd never seen them. He exited and turned left under the highway. Immediately he was into the lava field on his right with towering sandstone cliffs on his left. Within a mile he had left the sound of traffic and evidence of people behind. An old pickup truck passed, headed the way he had come, but Jeffers' car was the only one headed south.

"This is good. I'm betting cops aren't going to be watching this empty road. Hunting for me, they'll expect me to use a bigger road to get away fast. Not some low speed, winding little thing like this. OK, it's ten now, I can probably be in Mexico by sundown." Talking to himself helped keep him awake. Now that he was feeling safer, last night's lack of sleep was catching up with him.

"Need sleep! Too long watching so I could set the fire, then watching the damn firemen put it out, hell I was watching all night. I want a nap. I want a map! I want to know where I am."

Some miles back he passed an empty parking lot on his left, but hadn't thought to stop then. He didn't want to back track so he pulled over at the next wide spot and looked in the glove box. "F-it. I thought I had a map, but it's not here now. No problem, I'll use my phone."

He pulled it out of a pocket and turned it on. "No service?! What the hell good is this thing! Not only no service—no juice. It's damn near dead," Jeffers added as he realized he had so little power left. He hadn't been thinking about charging it lately. He took a drink of water and opened the pouch of jerky for a snack.

"Gotta keep going. Just aim south." He pulled back onto the road and washed down the salty meat with a hefty swig of water. Jeffers slowed as he approached a road junction. The road ahead went to Lehew, and the arrow to the right said Techado. Neither name meant anything to him, but south was straight ahead although the road was smaller.

"Smaller road, less chance of the police traveling it. That's good enough, and straight south as well, even better."

The quality of the road deteriorated with more potholes and rougher surface. He slowed some to compensate and not rattle himself too much. Even with the bumps, or maybe because of the rocking motion of the car, his eyelids drooped and he started drifting off. He was startled into wakefulness when his head fell forward in sleep and he snapped upright with a jolt.

The unwavering straight line of the road was mesmerizing, and his mind tired of chewing the same problem of escape over and over. He nodded gently and leaned against the head rest. *I see the road. I'm awake. I'm awake.* But he wasn't. The car veered slowly to the right and then faster down the slope into the arroyo at the base of the rumpled hills that flanked the road.

The abrupt stop, as the car buried its nose in the soft sand, threw his head against the steering wheel. Stars against blackness, then shocked awake and in pain with a bloody nose, Jeffers fumbled with the door handle and fell to the uneven ground outside the car.

"Fuck! OW!" Lurching to his feet, Jeffers touched his nose to see how much it was bleeding, and found it so painful he thought it was broken. There was a stack of shop towels on the back seat and he grabbed one to hold gently against his nose. "Damn! That hurts!" He got in the car, holding the towel and started the engine. When it caught, he put it in reverse and tried to back up the steeply angled side of the arroyo. The front wheels spun and dug the car in even deeper. *OK I get it. Not moving this baby without help. Fucking front wheel drive! I need a truck from the old motor pool. That'd get this baby out.* He clambered out of the car. The frame was resting on the ground so it was awkward, especially while using one hand to keep the towel on his nose.

The dry stream channel was only five feet deep, but it felt deeper as his feet slipped with each step upward. Reaching the road surface, he stopped and took the towel off. Gingerly, he felt his nose—just a little blood. "Good. Fuck, I left my water in the car. Oh well, there'll be someone by soon so I can hitch a ride. The sign said there was a burg out here somewhere, so I'll just walk down the road till I get there." Sweating, he wiped his face with the end of the towel. Jeffers was too tired and stressed for his stride to be jaunty, but it was determined.

The silence was broken only by the sound of his heavy tread. No birds were singing, no insects hummed. His mind went 'round and 'round his problem, with no satisfying solution. Mexico was not a happy ending for Jeffers. The quiet became oppressive. *Fuck! It is damned hot today.* He looked at his watch. "Might pay attention to how long it takes for a car to come down this road. Eleven thirty-seven. Nice rhyming number. Not yet noon." He smiled thinking that was how he would remember his walk. Talking to himself, "that steering wheel doesn't give much—except a hellacious headache. Ha! I'll walk it off. Damn it's scorching on this pavement. Bet it's cooler in the ditch and it'd be easier walking too. The slope is gentler here to get down there, why not? I can see the road and holler and wave when someone comes along."

No breeze ruffled the sagebrush as Jeffers slipped and slid down the several feet to the dry stream bed. He was still dressed in the work clothes from his shift at the warehouse on Monday, including heavy, steel-toed work boots. He found the sand was softer than he expected, and with his boots, harder to walk on than he anticipated. He refused to climb back up and kept his head down while slogging along. *How can sand be so frigging hot?* The arroyo had been slowly angling away from the road, and when he looked up, Jeffers realized he couldn't see the pavement any more. "No big deal. I know the road is just off to my left. I'm tired of this ditch. Gonna get back on the pavement. It was easier walking there after all. So what time is it? I must have walked a couple of miles already. Only twelve thirty? Fuck. Time doesn't fly when you are not having fun. That's a joke, fella."

Panting a bit, he regained ground level and plodded toward the road. A large pickup truck, windows up and music blaring so loud Jeffers could almost make out the words on the country song, zoomed by with the driver oblivious to Jeffers frantic waving and shouting a few hundred feet off to the side. A bout of coughing made him bend over. *Damn! My throat is so dry it hurts. And coughing didn't help my nose any either.* He choked some more. *Hard to swallow. Sure could use a cold beer. Good location for a bar. Hotter than Hades.* He licked his lips, making them sorer. *OK, onward to the road. Now I have proof that cars really use it. Fuck the pickup driver anyway. I'm not all that fond of country music.* He stumbled, but caught himself before he fell. "Speaking of pickups—pick up your feet oaf! Ha Ha! Another one of your stupid jokes? Yeah, well I have to do something for entertainment."

New Mexico's brilliant blue sky was unsullied by even a wisp of cloud, and the sun took full advantage of the opportunity to pour heat onto the landscape. Even as his sweat dried on his shirt, he soaked it again. Jeffers wasn't used to working outdoors, and riding a forklift didn't provide good exercise, so the lengthy walk was wearing him down. "I know there's a town this way—the pickup proved that, but Jeez am I thirsty. This place looks more like Afghanistan than Iowa. Right, you're not in Iowa anymore, Gordon. You left that behind long ago." Mumbling to himself, and stumbling along at the edge of the road, he kept putting one foot heavily in front of the other.

Tired, thirsty, so thirsty, hot, my head hurts, hard swallowing. His running litany of complaints was constant and became longer with every step.

He looked off to the right and saw shimmering water in the distance. "I know that's a mirage. No, it's a lake. It's wiggling like a mirage. What if it's not? I was walking in a stream bed. Where'd the water go? Downhill, dummy. It always goes downhill to a lake. See, that's what I said. It's a lake over there."

This internal dialogue continued. Finally Jeffers shouted, "I'll prove there's a lake there. I'm going to jump in it! Watch this," and he lurched off the road, which had become so hot it was burning his feet through his boots. Trudging toward the water in the distance, he intersected the arroyo once more. He slid down the now gently angling surface and slogged through the soft sand of the dry stream bed toward what his mind insisted was a lake.

Licking his lips in anticipation of the cool water to come, he tasted blood from a split lip. Staggering, he looked up to see someone leading the way. Blinking several times to clear his sight, he thought he recognized Rozlyn's back. "Rozlyn wait, wait for me to catch up, and we can walk to the lake together," he said as he stumbled trying to hurry. "Wait! I'm sorry I hit you. Just give me another chance." But the vision didn't slow. His feet dragged and refused to move any faster. The woman's head shook and she increased her lead, ignoring him. Jeffers' shoulders drooped and he shook with sobs as he tried to hurry after her.

Gasping, and falling to his knees on the blazing sand, catching himself with hands blistered by the heat, Jeffers whispered, "Rozlyn, please, come back, wait for me." The apparition turned and he saw her bony skull. Her skeletal jaw dropped open, but there were no words he recognized. The scream he heard was his own.

Chapter 12
TUESDAY—WEDNESDAY

Lanny fought to concentrate on her job, but concern about Jeffers' location, aftermath of the fire, and fatigue from the chaotic, sleepless night were catching up with her. "Come on Max, we're going home. I'm gonna chance it that Jeffers won't try something now. It's too soon after his failed fire for him to show up at my place again, but if so, I will sic you on him. I figure you'd like to sink your teeth into him, and I'd encourage you." She put the leash on Max, packed up a stack of papers, and explaining to the staff where she was going, left the law office.

Lanny opened her voice mail and heard Prez' confident message while parked in her driveway.

"Jeffers hasn't been spotted. We are assuming he's left town and is trying to disappear. He doesn't have much imagination and flying would not only subject him to scrutiny, it's expensive on short notice. It's probable he will head for Mexico by car. There are several places where he could cross the border without being concerned about the minimal guards. If he left his car in Columbus, he could simply walk across, since the Mexican side doesn't check for papers or a passport."

Cranky from fatigue, she wasn't so certain he was gone. "Yeah, you basing that on psychic ability mister detective? I hope you're right since I'm the one who'll pay the price if you're wrong," she said as she held the phone away from her ear and stared at it. Wishing there were a hand set to slam, like the ones on phones in old movies, she just poked the delete button vehemently and put the cell phone back in her pocket. A noise from the back seat reminded her. "Oh, sorry Max. That voice wasn't for you."

Standing at her back door, all the fear and adrenaline came surging back, and she surprised herself by bursting into tears again. *My poor place. Oh hell, why am I crying? ...damage is surficial.* She wiped her eyes with the back of her hand. *The important things are just fine. Pew. Glad the smoke isn't stronger. Fading, but still stinky. More airing, even if it is hot outside.* She raised the windows all around the house, and started a floor fan at the front door, after positioning Topper's old expandable gate across the opening. Max lay down in the breeze as though he had been there all his life. His tail thumped and his eyes closed as Lanny patted his head.

She spent time calling neighbors to thank them, and checking with insurers and small construction companies to see what all the repairs would cost. In spite of her concerns about Jeffers whereabouts, she was emotionally and physically exhausted early in the evening. She fed Max, let him through the gate into the back yard, made a scrambled egg, chile, and potato burrito, brought Max back in, locked her doors and fell into bed, where she slept uninterruptedly for more than eight hours.

A cold nose sniffing her hair, followed by soggy kisses on her forehead, eyes, and cheeks, was a rude awakening at seven on Wednesday morning. "Yuck, Max! Really. I love you too, but this isn't wonderful. You have morning breath." She laughed as she rolled out of bed, so his ploy worked. He trailed her as she padded to the kitchen, filled his bowl with food, and refreshed his water, and then refilled the hummingbird feeder and put water in the platform birdbath as well. "See Max, normalcy for us, even with the smoke smell still hanging on."

Later Prez texted her to make sure Max was okay, and see if they were getting along well. She smiled, realizing there was an ulterior motive in his texts. Even though she was self-sufficient, she had a warm response to having someone concerned about her well-being again.

Chapter 13
THURSDAY—FRIDAY

Thursday's text from Prez was blunt—body positively identified. Rozlyn Jeffers. Died from blow to back of head. Fell on sharp edge? Hit? Angle of injury suggests fall.

On Thursday when they went out to dinner at Prez's insistence, he told her the arrangement with her keeping Max was about to change.

Her face fell. Trying not to care, she waited to hear where Max would go, thinking of the strong bond already between her and the dog. Prez waited, knowing it wasn't what she wanted to hear before he told her Rozlyn's cousin would like to have Max, so her fostering days would be numbered. If she could manage it, Lanny could still have Max for another week or two until the cousin could arrange vacation days and travel from Ohio.

Prez texted to brief Lanny on Friday morning. Although the search had widened, there was still no news. Jeffers hadn't been seen anywhere and his vehicle was still unaccounted for.

Lanny, in tears, was putting her desk in order after staying late on a day that saw efforts on what she considered her pollution case, ignored. She was about to leave for the weekend, when her phone chirped with an incoming text. She glanced at it and seeing Prez's name, immediately called as requested.

"Hi Prez. What prompted the text? News?"

"Yeah, and it's about Jeffers. His car was spotted nose down in an arroyo south of the Malpais. It was invisible from the road, and if someone hadn't spotted a gleam off the side window from the curve, nearly a mile away, it could have stayed there a lot longer. No Jeffers. There was a package of jerky and a half empty water bottle in it. Current thinking is he hitched a ride south after crashing in the ditch. There are spots of blood on the steering wheel, maybe a head injury. No air bags in the early nineties, so he hit the wheel. This means the focus of the search has changed. Take Jeffers' Cutlass off the list. The team will go over it for evidence, but what they've found so far, only the usual trash of living in it. No hints as to where he might be, but the Ford is out there somewhere."

"That's not satisfying, but until he's under arrest, it's the best I get. I need an escape. Would you consider that worth celebrating with a drink and dinner after I feed Max?" Lanny asked while wiping her eyes with the back of her hand.

"You got it. You sound really down. See you in half an hour," Prez said, and hung up to file papers and lock his desk. Not yet lovers, they tiptoed toward intimacy.

Chapter 14
LATER

Another two weeks passed, with Jeffers receding into the background, as nothing was heard about him and there was no use of credit cards. The last time was the Tuesday of the fire when a sale at Love's on I-40 was recorded. This led to speculation he was in Mexico. A search of the nearby area was ordered and unsuccessful.

Lanny put Jeffers aside and concentrated on her work. Seeing her home being repaired, and feeling secure with Max as watch dog, fears of Jeffers started fading. She and Max were bonding even more, and it was like earlier years with her big German Shepherd. Walking in her neighborhood each evening was a happiness she had forgotten. Even though it was late in the season, there were still migrating birds and their songs and movement enhanced her walks. To no avail she told Max what bird was making which sound. He looked at her and wagged his tail, but it was obvious he was much more interested in the smells in the bushes.

Jeffers' case seemed over. Lanny and Prez talked about Jeffers thorough disappearance with irritation. Both wanted closure on the case, but with no new information, he didn't warrant much time. Prez always had something serious to worry over with the murder and robbery rates in Albuquerque, and what time was left over, they were spending together. He'd stopped finding excuses to call, and just assumed she expected to hear from him. She felt free to proffer invitations to dinner, or to suggest a baseball game, or a movie.

One Friday morning, Prez left a lengthy text message. "Not only a movie, but I'm offering chocolate and ProSecco afterward. Why don't you bring Max along too? I cook breakfast and that way you won't have to worry about him. A bag with his food and your toothbrush and I have everything else." Lanny listened to it several times during the day, noticing his slightly nervous tone and where he hesitated over a word, pleased that he was making a loving offer that was obviously something he didn't do every day.

After watching *When Harry Met Sally*, which was almost interrupted in the middle when Lanny got close enough for a kiss that more than equaled any one on the screen, and made them both recall the fake orgasm scene, she just snuggled under his arm and sniffled through the rest of the story.

When Prez turned off the set as the credits rolled, Lannie said, "Why don't we save the drinks and chocolate for later or another time? I have another endorphin creator to propose. This is why I've been watching nothing but swashbucklers and comedies. Movies that touch on loving make me aware that there are feelings I've ignored for too long."

"I'll give Max a treat and let him out. Don't move, I'll be right back."

Lanny almost did as she was told. While sitting still she unbuttoned the top two buttons on her blouse. Planning ahead when she got Prez's text, she was wearing her laciest bra, so she felt she was still leaving something to the imagination, and something for discovery. She also kicked off the sandals she'd been wearing and thought momentarily about unfastening her jeans skirt. Too obvious, she decided to wait.

"Max is happy and I think we are about to be as well." Prez offered a hand to help her off the couch; Lanny stepped forward, put her hand on his neck and gently pulled his face to hers. Her sensuous kiss said more than words as she leaned into him, responding to his kiss and full body hug.

When they came up for air, Prez held her shoulders and pushed her back so he could see her expression. He said, with a small smile, "I want to be sure we are on the same page. I haven't invited anyone to stay overnight like this in a long, long time...not talking about a platonic sleepover. Are you certain you want this commitment?"

"I thought my reaction would say enough, but if you're asking me if I want to make love with you tonight and have breakfast here in the morning, and see if we are at least best friends, I'll take the chance."

His smile broadened as he held her for another lengthy kiss, one hand caressing her back and wandering below her waist. Instead of turning her loose, he picked her up and carried her the few steps down the hall to his bedroom.

Prez set her down inside the doorway, "I'd like to help you get undressed. OK?" Lanny nodded, and stood still, watching his face as he struggled to undo the buttons on her blouse. He started to help her out of it. She turned away, shrugged and he held the empty shirt.

Grinning as she turned back to him, she said, "I can be a little helpful, if only to get to the sexy parts."

"Hey, I said I was out of practice...especially when it comes to women's buttons. Have you noticed they are backwards to men's. It's awkward."

"Excuses! My turn to help you out of a shirt. Where are you going to put my blouse so you can have empty hands? You can tell this place is lived in by a bachelor. The only chair is covered with clothes. Let's add another layer to it."

She followed him the few steps to the chair near a chest of drawers, and after unhesitatingly undoing his buttons, ran her hands inside the open shirt, caressing his body as she maneuvered to lift his shirt off his shoulders. Lanny dropped the shirt on the pile, and faced Prez with a smile, "Next? Your turn or do I get another one?"

Prez looked at her with exaggerated lust and a raised eyebrow, "I think I need a turn to redeem myself, although there doesn't look to be another row of difficult buttons. Maybe a hook or two, and I can handle zippers." He lifted one eyebrow at her, and twirled an invisible moustache as she coyly put one finger to her cheek and turned her back to him.

He unhooked the bra easily, and slid the straps down her arms till he could reach around her. "Forget the bra, this is a lot more interesting." He held her breasts while he closed the small space between them. She could feel his erection through his jeans and that, with her excitement from his caresses, electrified every nerve. She took a shuddering breath and turned in his arms so their bare torsos met. The kiss that followed stopped the joking as their desire overtook humor. Lanny unbuckled Prez's belt and unsnapped his jeans, then worked on her skirt while he kicked off his Tevas and shed his jeans.

They were suddenly hesitant when both stood there in underpants, her bikini lacy and black, his navy blue briefs with an obvious bulge.

Breaking the almost award silence, Prez said, "I knew you were beautiful, but I wasn't prepared for how sexy you are." He held out his hand. Lanny stepped forward and let herself be led the few steps to the bed. Prez tossed the spread off and lay down, beckoning her to join him. Lying down so they weren't staring at one another, eased the minor embarrassment, and brought back the original electricity. Prez rolled on his side and propped up on one elbow, leaned over and hungrily kissed Lanny. Her slightly open-mouthed, slightly damp, barely sucking return jolted him as if he'd touched a live wire. She added to the wattage by fondling his member through the thin cotton of pants. He was nuzzling her breast when her fingers found the fly opening and rubbed his length. His quiet moan of pleasure told how it affected him.

"Prez, I hate to be clinical, but do you have a condom somewhere nearby? We want loving, but I'm not ready for a family."

"Agreed, and you can reach them from your side of the bed. Drawer in the nightstand. I was going to get one, but you're nearer." Prez was shimmying out of his underwear as he spoke, and then he stroked Lanny's back from shoulder to cheeks as she stretched for the drawer. "Hmmm, I'm not sure if that is helping or hindering. It certainly is a distraction. You can stop that in an hour or two."

Prez gently snapped the elastic on her panties, "You're overdressed for this party. May I help?" She raised her hips while he eased the bikinis off and nuzzled her froth of pubic hair. "You even smell like lavender here." He lightly massaged her mons and reached between her legs as she stroked his erection and then unrolled a condom over it.

Leaning over again, he ran his tongue around her nipple and softly sucked it for a finale. He rolled on his back and pulled her onto his hips. She felt his length and heat under her, lifted slightly and wiggled his insertion. Her sigh and his gasping deep breath said how well they fit together. He grabbed her hips and rocked them as one. Lanny braced her hands on his ribs and pushed back against his motion, gasping with pleasure. Prez bent his knees and provided back support.

He opened his eyes and held her still. Lanny looked at him to understand the change, and in response to the question in her eyes, before she asked him if something was wrong, he did a move that made her gasp as he used his core strength to turn them over.

With just a slight adjustment, he could support himself and have one hand free to caress her breast as he leaned forward to resume his motion. Lanny wrapped one leg over his so she could push him deeper. He reacted instantly, thrusting again, and again; with a soft moan, she met him with her force and need, until his climax triggered hers and left them depleted but satiated. All they could do for several minutes was try to catch their breath.

Braced on his arms, Prez whispered in Lanny's ear. "Whoever said chocolate was as good as sex was wrong. Really wrong." She smiled happily as she turned her head to kiss him. He rolled off, kissed her again and said, "Be right back" and went into the bathroom.

He returned a few minutes later wearing a towel sarong slung around his hips. He found Lanny with the covers pulled up to her nose, rather than on them. "I agree, dang, it's cold in here. A/C either hot or too cold." He dropped the towel on the bed and joined her under the covers.

"I have a few things to care for before calling it a night. My turn to leave this nest." She padded to the living room, found her bag with shortie nightgown, and toothbrush, let Max back in, finished ablutions and scrambled back to the bed. Max followed, curled up at the foot of the bed, yawned and went to sleep. So did Lanny and Prez.

Breakfast was not anticlimactic; it quietly solidified their growing intimate relationship. They teased one another and enjoyed the simple domestic actions of preparing a meal and eating it together.

Sharing a bed and intimacy added depth to a relationship that had been growing on a friend and semi-professional level since Lanny was still hoping for closure on Max's case, as she had come to think of it. Their closeness also gave her a sympathetic ear and a thoughtful response when she voiced her dissatisfaction with attitudes at the attorney's office.

⸙

Her body language and what Prez thought of as a glow of success, radiated from her as she joined him at the Flying Star for an early dinner before a concert. She was nearly bouncing with energy all through the meal, but saved her announcement for dessert and coffee.

"In what I'm considering emotional compensation for being shuffled off the major pollution case, the secondary one I was working on for the last six months, just settled out of court—hugely in my client's favor. I'm getting enough bonus money to think about another trip to Panama. Would you like to come with me? If you say yes, I'll get busy with when and how." Lanny smiled over her cup of coffee.

"With you? Of course. I like what you've said about it and I want to see for myself all the interesting places. There's lots of details to saying yes, but the desire is there. Give me a few options on timing and a couple days to see if I can arrange time off."

⸙

Then a Duke City Towing Company driver was referred to Prez by an officer in another division. "We were called to the Sunport long term parking lot. A car there had a flat tire. It had a tumbleweed caught underneath it and the windshield was dirty. It must have been there a while. My boss listens to the police band and something rang a bell. He keeps a list of stolen and wanted vehicles. We don't want trouble. Anyway, this car is a white Ford Fiesta and the plate is MMW178."

"Hang on a sec. Let me check my list." Prez responded. "Yeah, that's one we'd like to check thoroughly. Drag it to the impound yard."

When Prez got to the yard, the print guys were already finished and he was free to go over it. Donning gloves, he opened the glove box and leafed through the papers. Registration was to Rozlyn Jeffers as he anticipated. He found an old pay stub, a pack of tissues, a tin of mints, a lipstick melted onto an expired coupon book from the local public radio station, and the owner's manual for the 2002 model. *Nothing worth writing home about.* He peered under the seats, and looked in the back, and found no evidence of violence. *Well, one more piece of the puzzle is in place.* He relocked the doors and signed out of the yard.

He called Lanny and shared the Fiesta information. "My guess is he was trying, poorly, to make us think she'd flown somewhere. Maybe he thought the suitcase would go in lost luggage and disappear. Who knows? At this stage, I don't much care until we arrest him. Then I'll ask." Prez said.

"I agree. He wasn't thinking smartly or intelligently through all this. Even the murder was probably more an accident than something done with evil intent or malice. It was tragic for Rozlyn and just sad. It shouldn't have occurred," Lanny said.

"Yeah, the state of the house, with empty beer cans filling the trash can, along with various empties of tequila and rum, with a fridge in the garage still loaded with beer and mixers, tells me some serious drinking was going on. That magnifies personal difficulties. The brochures and books about PTSD have me convinced he came back from Afghanistan with problems he couldn't handle. Whatever, he couldn't control his life."

Chapter 15
A SUNDAY

"I'm glad you're with me. Between dealing with house repairs and the frustrating court case, it's been over three months since I've been up here. It's fun to share you with friends, and I love introducing you to this. You get to have your first lesson next week and then Panama!" Lanny said this while standing, holding the steering bar. "You'll want to step back, and I'll see you down below." Prez gave her a quick kiss, and a thumbs up. He watched her run four steps and leap off the mountain.

"Oof," she gasped as the harness tightened, and she leaned into position to soar. The wing caught air and steadied. She smiled, the joy of flying returning. Lanny glanced up at the wing overhead. The blue and gray bands enhanced the arrow shape of the hang glider, and she loved its elegance. She inhaled deeply and settled into the straps.

The Sandia Mountains, rugged, beautiful, loomed on her left. She was comforted by their stability, unaltered for tens of thousands of years. She breathed in the aroma of dusty pines, and laughed out loud, happily considering the unexpected changes in her life.

She found a good updraft and made a circle, taking some time on her way south to the meeting spot. *Lots of sirens. Miserable Tijeras Canyon strikes again. Any accident in that stretch of highway shuts it down. Bet Prez is caught in whatever has the police and EMTs on their way. No matter, I'll wait for him at the soccer field.*

~∾∽~

Albuquerque Journal, On Sunday, July 17, Homicide Detective Scott Preston (Prez), 40, a twelve-year member of the Albuquerque Police Department, was killed instantly while directing traffic through a multi-car, multi-semi accident on I-40 in Tijeras Canyon. Although the van he was driving was not involved, when he encountered the scene, he stopped to render aid to a seriously injured elderly man. He was directing traffic away from the 11 vehicle pile-up when he was struck by a passing truck. Preston is survived by a sister in Oregon. See Rio Grande Funerals and Cremations website for more information regarding Memorial Service.

THE END

Acknowledgments

The author would like to thank many friends and experts for making this novella better. Jim Tritten, my frequent co-author, this time proffered ideas and encouragement as I wrote solo. Don Reightley who flew hang gliders off the Sandias, checked the details regarding accuracy about flying. His willingness to share his knowledge enriched the story. I am grateful for the Corrales Writing Group's gentle criticism and positive reinforcement which strengthens my writing. Other good friends, especially Freda McKeown, and Mikal Deese offered additional comments and reassurance that the story was worth reading. Finally, the support and help from my long-time spouse Richard is irreplaceable.

About the Author

Sandi Hoover is a geologist by training and naturalist by interest. She enjoys watching and writing about the behavior of wildlife, trying to understand how they fulfill their basic needs. Human emotions and their expression also stimulate stories. Indulging her curiosity about nature has inspired trips to experience wilderness firsthand. From King Eiders in Barrow, Alaska, to King Penguins on South Georgia Island, seeing animals in their natural habitat has been a life-long pursuit. She is a member of the award winning Corrales Writing Group, and an award winning author in her own right.

Sandi spent her working career as executive director of the Houston Audubon Society and then the Bayou Preservation Association, both active conservation non-profit organizations. While those positions led to interesting activities, her writing was specific and pragmatic. There was no humor or fiction involved in position papers and environmental statements. Her writing as an avocation has been one of growth and discovery.